TAYLOR R

M000105600

&

The Seeds of Wisdom

Story by Sully

Illustrations by John Carrozza

To Emmett

From Farmer Smolak 2019

"Integrity is our greatest asset"™

Published by:

PAINTED HORSE PUBLICATIONS, Inc.
Haverhill, MA

978-373-2927   smolakfarms@stopforastory.com

"*Integrity is our greatest asset*"™

ISBN 0-9708066-0-4

Text and illustrations ©1994
Painted Horse Publications, Inc. All rights reserved including
the right of reproduction in whole or any part in any form.
Original printing 1994
Reprinted 1998, 2001

I dedicate this story to Keith Sliney.
Although his name is not on the cover, his efforts
have made this all possible.

To Coleen, Kelly, Kyle, Taylor and Rachel
I dedicate my life.
~ *Sully*

For Henry and Dorothy.
~ *J.C.*

Special Thanks to:
Mike Giorgi
Barbara Whitmore
Everyone at Smolak's Farm
Georgetown Savings

$\mathcal{I}$nside the brown and gray fieldstone walls that surrounded Smolak's Farm, just south of the duck pond and right beside the pumpkin patch was a burrow. Under the burrow lived a colony of rabbits.

The rabbits had chosen this place to live for one reason and one reason alone. They chose this spot because it looked out over the pumpkin patch and the rabbits certainly loved pumpkins. In fact, pumpkins were their favorite food.

It was a cool fall evening, and all the rabbits sat at the edge of the thicket eating pumpkins and pumpkin seeds. For as much as the rabbits loved pumpkins, they loved the seeds more.

Crunch, crunch, crunch, was the sound the seeds made as Taylor Rabbit ate them. As he munched on his seeds, Taylor looked out over the pumpkin patch and in a day-dreamy sort of way thought about how wonderful the seeds were. *Out of one tiny seed, come a bunch of big, bright orange pumpkins and all of them are full of seeds. How wonderful!*

"Hey, Taylor! You sure can pack away a bunch of seed for such a little rabbit!" yelled Lightning Rabbit, who stood close by with his friends Quicken and Jack.

"Where do you put all that seed, Taylor?" asked Quicken. "You eat as much as any rabbit your age, yet you are only half their size. What is your secret, friend Taylor?" The three rabbits laughed about Taylor, his size and amount of seed that he ate.

Suddenly, a stern voice interrupted their laughter. "What's going on here?" King Rabbit asked. He ruled the colony sternly, but fairly. Quicken, Lightning and Jack were quiet, for they knew that King Rabbit treated all the rabbits fairly and he had no tolerance for teasing. "I'll say it again. What's going on here?"

"Ah, nothing sir," fibbed Jack Rabbit. Quicken and Lighting quickly bobbed their heads in agreement.

"Taylor?"

"Oh, nothing sir. We were just discussing how wonderful the seeds are and how all those huge orange pumpkins start from just one seed."

"Ah yes, the seeds are a wonderful thing," said King Rabbit. "And their abundance should not be taken for granted. Indeed, they should be cherished. Isn't that right boys?" he said, nodding toward Quicken, Lightning and Jack.

"Yes sir, King Rabbit!" the three said.

"Well then, finish your seed and then head for the burrow. It's getting late."

Taylor watched King Rabbit hop away. He noticed something different in the King. There was an unnatural tightness in his brow and Taylor sensed concern. The King would have to choose a new leader soon and all the rabbits wondered who it would be.

"Thanks Taylor Rabbit, for not telling King Rabbit of our teasing," said Lightning.

"Sorry, Taylor Rabbit," said Jack, "our teasing was uncalled for."

"That's OK," Taylor said (although he really didn't mean it). Quicken, Lightning and Jack were his friends, but when they teased him, it really hurt Taylor's feelings.

Quicken hopped over to Taylor and put his paw around him. "Friend Taylor, what you lack in strength you surely make up for in brains, and there is much to be said for that. Just look at King Rabbit. He was never a big rabbit, but he certainly is the wisest."

A smile came across Taylor's face. Quicken, Lightning and Jack were truly his friends. Taylor's hurt feelings were forgotten as the group of young rabbits hopped back into the burrow.

The next morning when Taylor awoke, he sniffed the air in his room and knew that rain was falling on the fields above. Taylor didn't like rainy days very much.

Knock, knock, knock. Taylor rolled off his mattress of field hay and answered the door. It was Marshal Rabbit. Marshal Rabbit was King Rabbit's messenger.

"Good morning, Taylor Rabbit," said Marshal. "I have been sent to tell you of an announcement by King Rabbit to be made in the main burrow. Please be there."

"I will be there," Taylor said, and Marshal quickly hopped off to inform the others.

When Taylor arrived in the main burrow, all the rabbits were there. He sat down next to Quicken, Lightning and Jack just as King Rabbit started to speak.

"My fellow rabbits," King Rabbit began, "I'm afraid that the pumpkin patch has become very dangerous. I smell three dogs instead of the one we have known. You all know the nature of dogs is to chase rabbits and this is a dangerous problem." A look of concern was on every rabbit's face.

"The dogs never go beyond the walls of the farm. We must gather pumpkins from the field and store seeds in the burrow this winter. In the spring, we will become like farmers ourselves, and plant a pumpkin patch in the clearing outside the fieldstone wall. This will call for sacrifice. We will now only eat half the seeds we gather. We will store the other half for spring. Quicken, Lightning and Jack Rabbit will go to the fields today and gather the pumpkins, for tomorrow it will be even more dangerous."

"I'll go too! I can help!" Taylor Rabbit was standing and waving his paws in the air.

"Thank you for the offer, Taylor Rabbit, but Quicken, Lightning and Jack are the strongest and fastest rabbits. They will be best for this job. Your time to help will come later."

Taylor Rabbit sank into his seat. More than anything, he wanted to help.

Quicken, Lightning and Jack Rabbit did their job well. They returned from the fields, telling stories of how they outsmarted the farmer's new dogs. They had plenty of pumpkins too.

That night after dinner, all the rabbits in the burrow separated the pumpkin seeds. Half they put in storage, and half they saved to be eaten.

Fall became winter, and the rabbits settled in for a long winter sleep. The pumpkins were gone from the fields. The ducks had flown south and a blanket of white covered the earth. The farm was asleep for the winter.

Everything was quiet until the first sign of spring. Taylor Rabbit woke from his long winter rest and the first thing he thought of was the pumpkin seeds.

Taylor decided to hop down the hall to the storage room door and take a sniff of the pumpkin seeds. What better way to start the spring? He smiled because he was the first of all the rabbits to rise from the winter nap.

As he neared the storage room door, Taylor stopped suddenly and let out a small gasp. The door was open! Taylor's eyes widened as he slowly hopped closer. "This shouldn't be. This just shouldn't be," Taylor said to himself as he neared the door. He didn't really want to look inside, but he knew that he had to.

Creeeeeek, the door sounded as Taylor pushed it open. Taylor took a deep breath, closed his eyes and took one short hop into the room. The aroma of seed was very weak. Taylor slowly opened his eyes.

There was not a seed in sight. "Oh my goodness. Where could all the wonderful magical seeds have gone?" Taylor said as he hopped around the empty room.

Then Taylor took one more strong sniff, and that's when he saw them. Tucked away in the farthest corner of the room. Taylor Rabbit spotted a paw full of seed.

"Oh gracious me, they didn't all disappear!" said Taylor happily. He hopped over and picked up the seed in his trembling paw. They smelled so good that his first thought was to eat them. But Taylor used his wisdom to overcome temptation.

"No, no, no," Taylor said to himself, "I mustn't eat these seeds. If I do, there will be no pumpkin patch. I will take them to King Rabbit so that we can start our garden as planned."

Taylor hopped quickly to the King's chamber and burst through the door without knocking. This was something that no rabbit was allowed to do. As the door burst open, Taylor tripped and the seeds that he held spilled all over the floor.

The King was shocked at Taylor's sudden entrance. "What on earth are you doing, Taylor Rabbit?" exclaimed the King. Then he noticed the seeds.

At the same moment, Marshal Rabbit hopped frantically into the King's chamber. "Oh my ... oh my dear ... the seeds ...gone...gone ... every last one." Marshal was out of breath and obviously very upset. "I fear that someone has eaten all the seeds!" Marshal and the King both looked at the seeds on the floor and then at Taylor.

"Oh no, no," said Taylor Rabbit. "I did not eat all the seeds. When I went to the storage room, these were the only seeds left."

"The evidence is right in front of us," said Marshal Rabbit.

King Rabbit was silent for a long moment. Then he said, "What appears to be true is not always the truth. Taylor Rabbit did not eat the seed, he is still thin. Thank you Taylor for saving the seeds so that we may start our pumpkin patch. Marshal Rabbit, I would like you to gather the other rabbits in the main burrow at once."

Word of the missing seed had spread quickly.

When King Rabbit appeared in the burrow with Taylor Rabbit at his side, all the other rabbits whispered among themselves. Then King Rabbit started to speak.

"My fellow rabbits. It seems that over this past winter, there were those among us that could not wait. They ate all the seeds that we had stored for the spring. However, thanks to Taylor Rabbit, a handful of seeds were saved. We will be able to start our pumpkin patch as planned, although it will be much smaller."

"We owe a great debt of gratitude to Taylor. As for the thieves, they shall be punished."

"I have asked Taylor Rabbit what the punishment for the thieves should be, and he has decided. They shall be put in charge of tending the garden. The work of cultivating the soil, planting the seed and weeding the garden will be theirs," said King Rabbit. "For one year, these rabbits will not have the privilege of eating the seed that they grow. Taylor's sentence is fair. He has become the wisest rabbit in the burrow. I have decided Taylor Rabbit will be our new King.

All the rabbits stood, clapping and cheering for their new leader. They all agreed that Taylor should be their new King.

One cool day the next fall, King Taylor sat on the brown and gray fieldstone wall and looked out over the pumpkin patch. All his friends had worked extremely hard at making the patch a success. *How magical*, thought King Taylor. *Out of only a handful of seeds grew all these big, bright orange pumpkins. How wonderful.*

Then he heard a voice. "How in the world did all these pumpkins get on this side of the wall?" said Farmer Smolak. Taylor Rabbit looked up at the farmer. It was then that Farmer Smolak knew that this small rabbit was responsible for the pumpkin patch outside the wall. Farmer Smolak tipped his hat to Taylor and said "Fine job, sir rabbit. Fine job indeed."

Taylor Rabbit and Farmer Smolak both knew that it is as important to give to nature as it is to take.

The End.

A Brief History

Smolak Farm sits on 160 acres in North Andover, Massachusetts. It has become a Merrimack Valley  landmark by combining agriculture, education, and entertainment in a very unique way. The Farm's landscape was sculpted by prehistoric glaciers, and its rolling hills now provide a home for peach, plum, and apple orchards, as well as a Christmas tree farm and a pumpkin patch.

The Smolak Farms setting provided inspiration for local author Bill "Sully" Sullivan, who's first book *Taylor Rabbit and the Seeds of Wisdom* is set on the farm. Smolak Farms and Painted Horse Publications, Inc. have teamed up to provide the public twenty books over five years set on or about the farm. This coupling of a superior environment with quality literature is our joint effort to provide enrichment for young minds.